THE TEACHER

JOSEPH FASANO

A MAUDLIN HOUSE BOOK

MAUDLIN H✦USE

maudlinhouse.net
twitter.com/maudlinhouse

The Teacher
Copyright © 2025 by Joseph Fasano
ISBN 979-8-9923773-2-3

for Leonardo

The man had sand in his eyes. He had traveled for five days through the desert, and there were times when he was so lost in his own mind that he forgot he was not alone. A mule's breath soothed his shoulder as it followed him, and when he turned back he saw the woman riding in the saddle.

"We are never alone," she'd said to him before they left, "so long as we have each other."

The man stopped and brushed the sand from his eyebrows and turned back and helped the woman down from the saddle.

The mule knelt in the sand. The two travelers huddled beside it out of the wind. The man laid his hand on the woman's belly and looked up into her eyes.

"Soon," he said, "we'll be three."

As the winds swirled, the woman slept. The man held her against his chest and began to speak to the child.

He had thought that he would say wise things, lessons he had learned in his hard life, but he heard himself, instead, asking questions.

"Who will you be?" "Why did you come to me and your mother?" "What story will our lives be now?"

They reached the town by first light. Like any father, the man believed there would be stories told about how his child was born, but in truth the world was passing them by: strangers' faces in the streets, morning's vendors carrying their wares, even the starlight draining from the sky.

He found them a small shelter and shouldered some horses aside and made a place for the woman to lie down. No visitors came, no one to bring gifts or fortune. There was only the sound of the wind moving through the loose slats of the shelter.

"I could fix those," the man thought, for he had been a craftsman since the days of his youth, as his father had been, and his father's father before him.

"I could fix those." He heard his father's voice in his

mind now, that voice that had said so many strange things to him in the darkness: "We cannot remake what we cannot love," it had said. "Love is not a shelter from ourselves."

The woman lay in the hay the man had gathered for her. It was a new pain that she felt now, and she let herself into it slowly, like a child clinging to the bank of a river, wading in, unsure of what would happen.

She closed her eyes and saw scenes from her life. Young as she was, there were so many: a house on fire, a boy standing in a room with a bowl of fresh milk, her mother dismantling a loom after her father had died.

She felt something moving through her, like floodwater through a house, and she knew it would be different from how she had imagined it; she was not the swimmer lowering herself into the waters of what was happening; she was the waters themselves.

The child came into the light as his mother was told she herself had come: fighting, at first, and then wild to grasp at the world. The man cut the cord that bound mother and child and laid the child on her breast and covered them with the soft cotton of his tunic.

"We're blessed it is not cold," she said.

"Shhh," the man crooned, laying his hand on her forehead. "You must rest."

The woman looked down at her child, whose eyes were still closed. She recalled something strange from her childhood: Her father had woken her, once, in the night, and led her to the dark barn and told her to kneel beside a white mare in the moonlight. The mare was writhing in her labor pains, and when the foal finally arrived, her father laid it over the mare's shoulders and shook his head. "Death, too," he said, "like any of us, fights to be born."

A bolt of fear ran through the woman as she remembered this, but she looked down again at her child and watched him open his eyes. The irises were the color of bright honey, a hint of darkness at their edges, like the honey the bees made in the country of her youth, darkened by heather and rue. The man was kneeling beside her. He still had sand in his hair.

"What shall we name him?" she whispered.

"We should name him," he said, "for the place where we made him."

The man would only later come to know that we are not the makers of the lives of others.

"We are only poor merchants," the woman said,

"but this boy is our Light."

"Solé," he said, for the name meant Light in their tongue.

The woman nodded, and very softly she began to wipe the sand from the child's hair.

Solé grew strong. He ate good bread his mother made each week, and he drank fresh milk, and he was nourished by what his parents said the world was.

"No Gods ask us to fear them," his mother told him, and his father always nodded. "You will decide in your time what Gods there are, but all I know is a child who is raised only to fear God or Gods will always fear himself." His mother touched his face when she said this. "The child who is raised with love," she said, "does not see the face of beauty as a mask."

His mother died in his seventh year. Her illness was quick but very painful. In the final days, Solé knelt on one side of her bed, and his father knelt on the other, and they held hands over his mother's body. His father said words he could not understand, and when men came to carry his mother from the house, he did not weep. A week later, he was sweeping the dust from the kitchen, and he learned that we never know what we are feeling. When the kitchen floor was clean, he laid the broom in the corner, by his mother's loom, and fell to his knees and wept until the moon rose.

He stood in his father's workshop for hours, watching him work. When his father was thirsty, he brought him fresh water from the well, which smelled of iron from the deep earth. Already Solé had begun to feel strange sensations. He would feel his tongue parched long before his father asked him for water. And he would hear a voice inside him saying, *I thirst.*

"Tell me the story," he said one morning, "of how I was born."

His father laid the hammer down on a plank and brushed the sawdust from his hands.

"We were on a journey," his father said.

"I know. But to where?"

"You've heard this story before." His father smiled as he turned back to his work. "But I will tell it."

Solé sat on a pile of uncut wood and crossed his ankles.

"There was no destination," his father said. "All we knew was that we could not stay where we had been."

"Why, Papa?"

"It had become no place in which to live."

Often his father would speak like this, and always Solé understood there was some great truth behind the telling. But his father would only look away and smile.

"Come," his father said, "help me with this." He was holding out the hammer with one hand, bracing a board with the other.

Solé stepped forward and took the hammer. He slipped a nail from between his father's lips and placed it at the edge of the board, where his father was joining it.

"Tap softly at first."

Solé placed the tip of the nail in the soft grain of the wood and tapped its head three times until it nestled there.

"Very good," his father said, "very good."

They worked together often, and Solé's favorite things to make were the toy horses that his father would sell to the merchants from Divara, from Zuzanna, from Boacea. Solé liked to imagine them in the hands of young children, perhaps children who had never had such things in their lives. To Solé, the horse seemed an image of everything he loved: so strong, so wild, and yet somehow broken. "Perhaps," his father had said once, when they were speaking of horses, "perhaps our hearts are like that, too."

They made tables, chairs, even small boats that fishermen would come and carry off on their shoulders. But recently his father's face had grown weary with sleeplessness. A visitor had come in the night, his father told him, and given them a great task.

"What is it?" Solé asked. He was eleven now, and although he was very slender, his hands were large and his back was straight, and he could speak as clearly as the wind sings. For his mother had been a lover of books, and always she had read to him in the nights.

"I don't know," his father said, "what the task is. But I know how it begins."

"Papa, why are you always confusing me?"

His father spilled some pieces of wood onto the workbench and shook his head. "These won't do," he said. "And we'll need steel, maybe from the scraps in the shipyard. And eagle feathers, from the nests up in the hills."

He turned to Solé. "Do you think you could find those?"

"Feathers and steel," Solé said. "We're making arrows, aren't we?"

His father was squinting at the pieces of wood. "Whatever story this is, Solé, that's how it begins. And we don't have much time."

In ten days they had finished their work, and Solé's father woke him before the sun rose and said they were going on a journey.

"Where, Papa?"

"We don't just make things," his father said. "We have to sell them."

Solé rubbed the sleep from his eyes. "But what about the men who come and gather what we've made and bring it all to Divara." Divara was the name of a city far to the North, where merchants sold their wares and other things happened, strange things that Solé could sense he was not supposed to know.

"Yes," his father said, but sooner or later a maker must show his face."

Solé did not understand.

"Come," his father said, "help me load the wagon."

They were traveling a full day when Solé began to weep. His father took him down from the wagon and sat him in the sand and thumbed the hair from his eyes. He lifted a small metal flask and helped Solé drink for a long time.

The mule was digging at the sand, and Solé lifted the flask to its lips and then watched his father pour some water into his hands so the animal could drink.

Father and son sat in the sand and watched the sun sinking on the horizon.

"Will we be there in time?" Solé asked.

"Yes," his father said. "Whenever we arrive, it will be in time."

Solé's head was heavy, and he leaned forward and let his father wrap a cotton scarf around his eyes, to keep him safe from the wind.

"Are you afraid?"

Solé moved his head, but his father could not tell if it was a yes or a no.

"Perhaps we should have a lesson."

"I'd like that very much."

"Then we shall have a lesson on love. What better thing to warm our hearts as these winds howl and this sand burns?"

"Yes, Papa."

"Very good. Close your eyes."

"They are closed."

"Very good. Very good."

Lesson 1: LOVE

I tell you these things, Solé, so that you can keep them when I am gone. In time, you will be the one teaching me.

But for now, this is how it is. It's a funny thing that your grandparents chose to name me Aldo, a name that had never been in our family, a name that means its bearer should be wise. That name has kept me humble.

I am no wiser than the least wise of men, but I have lived many years in this world, and if a person lives with eyes and ears and heart open, he cannot help but learn.

We learn to carry our lives, each of us in his own

way. I have thought about that often in my journey. If someone were suddenly asked to have my life, he would crumble under its weight, for he would not have had a lifetime to learn to carry it. And it is the same way with me. I would not be able to carry the life of another, if suddenly I had to become it. Let that be a thought that humbles us, always. When you look into the eyes of another, tell yourself you do not know what he is carrying. You do not know what a victory every breath of a stranger is.

I promised to talk to you about love, my child, and perhaps I already am.

One day there will come into your life a great joy, and you will call it sorrow. Or one day there will come into your life a great sorrow, and you will call it joy. These are the two sentences with which a love story begins.

In my days I have learned one thing about love, and your mother would tell you the same. Every life is a ghost story. Every life is led by what it doesn't know it loves.

Let me tell you a story: a long time ago, two armies were at war. One army was trying to break into the city of the other. Try as they might, they could not do it. Their soldiers, far from home, despaired. Their generals held their heads in shame.

War is a wicked thing, my child, and I will speak of that in time. But you must take the story that I am telling and find the truth in it, beyond the shields and the armor and the steel.

The Greeks—for that is who they were—had burned their ships in the harbor, before the great city of Troy. This was their way of saying to their enemies, and to themselves, there is no turning back.

And yet they labored in vain to enter the city.

So Odysseus, a strange man among them, had an idea. What if we give them a gift? The soldiers looked at him in astonishment. But he went on. What if we give them a great wooden horse, built from the trees of the shore and the staves of our boats that have washed up in the sands? Still his compatriots looked at him in astonishment. Hear me out, he said. We will build this thing, and we will leave it at the gates of the city, and then we will disappear over the hills to the South.

So we will give up? A soldier said.

No, Odysseus said, we will hide inside our gift.

This story has been told many times, and much better than I am telling it, my child. But I tell it now to you because you must see that it is a story about trust. And this is the great question in any heart. What do I trust? What do I admit? Whom do I let in?

The answers to such questions are not like the answers to problems of geometry, the problems a craftsman can solve. They are different for every life. And you will have to be a ruined city many times, many times, before you let the right gift into your life.

But I will tell you what the Trojans did not do. They did not listen.

As with all stories, there is a detail of this story that is never told. And yet it is the heart of the lesson:

It is said that there was a wise man in the city of Troy. When the great wooden horse was wheeled inside the gates, this man, who was blind, and who walked with a wooden cane, felt his way toward the strange new thing and laid his ear against it. The horse was so large that the man's ear touched only its ankle, but he listened closely, and his face had the look of one who is remembering something from long ago.

The Trojans hurried this man away, for what was he except a blind pauper in rags? Surely he had no wisdom to offer them.

The story is one you will hear often: the gift that the people had let into their city was no gift at all. As soon as the citizens slept, the Greek soldiers climbed out of their wooden horse and razed the city. Few were spared.

In the seventh hour of the night, a Greek soldier came upon the old, blind man. He was sitting at the table of his little home, eating a loaf of bread and drinking a glass of milk. Before the soldier slew him, the old man shook his head and said, *This. This is the fate of those who do not listen.*

So it is with love, my child. We never know whom we are letting into the gates of our lives. But our work is to understand their hearts. Like the old man, you must lean in and listen to what is within, and you will find, again and again, that a person who stands before your life is telling you, as clear as day, exactly who they are. If you only listen.

We are on a journey now, Solé. Soon I will tell you where we are going. But for now I will only hold you as you sleep, and lay my hand on your heart, and listen to your breath.

I have told you, in this little tale, to listen to the

hearts of others. But I have learned something else, my child. We must turn that ear to ourselves. We must listen to what is waiting in our own hearts.

For we can betray ourselves more brutally than any enemy at the gates.

Aldo had fallen asleep with Solé in his arms. The sand had gathered around them in the night, and they woke only when the mule stirred and stood, raining more sand upon them.

Aldo laughed. "It's not in your eyes, is it, Solé?"

"No, Papa."

"Good. I had the most marvelous dream, and there was a horse in it, and perhaps this mule of ours took offense to that. Perhaps he wanted to prove that no matter what we dream, we always wake into the world. And the world is better than any dream."

"I'm still tired, Papa."

"I know, Solé. But we'll need water soon. And the oasis is another day's journey."

"I wish Mama were here."

"I do, too."

"I thought you were going to say, 'Perhaps she is.'"

"No, Solé. Fathers get tired too. There are times when I can't believe that."

Solé looked at the open desert before them. He was very thirsty.

"What if we don't reach the oasis?"

"We will."

Solé thought for a long time. Then he said, "I think Mama will help us get there."

"Then you must think that, my child. Do not take a belief from yourself just because someone else cannot believe it."

"I do believe it."

"Good," his father said. "Very good."

They were traveling for half a day when the axle of the wagon broke. The mule balked, and Aldo calmed it with his large hands. He made his way to the wagon and knelt down and inspected the axle.

"Can you fix it, Papa?"

"I think so. I have you to help me now."

They worked for a long while as the sun took its place at the zenith. Aldo stripped a leather cord from one of the mule's saddle bags and wrapped it around the crack in the axle. Then he asked Solé to pull one of the ribs from the wagon.

The canvas bowed where the rib had been. Together, they straightened the rib and broke it in two. Aldo tossed one half into the wagon, and he asked Solé to hold the other half along the length of the axle. He wove more of the leather cord around it and tied the cord with a knot he had learned in his childhood, when his father had taken him fishing on the sea.

"There," he said, standing up in the sunlight. The wind had fallen, and the air was very hot and very dry.

"Do you think it will hold, Papa?"

"We can only hope."

They traveled again until sunset. Surely the road must be near, Aldo thought, but he did not want to worry Solé by saying it aloud. He walked beside the mule, since he did not want to strain the bandaged axle, and Solé rode in the driver's seat, bundled in linens his mother had woven many years ago. My son, Aldo thought, is only the weight of a sawhorse. He is so thin, just as I am. We must make our way soon to the road. We must eat.

Aldo thought Solé was sleeping, but as the sun fell on the horizon, flooding the sands with a crimson light, he heard his son's voice.

"Papa, you said a word back there I've wondered about often."

"I knew you would ask about it, Solé. Go ahead and say it."

"Hope."

Aldo did not stop walking. He held the lead of the mule's halter and lowered his face against the wind, which had strengthened with the falling of the sun.

"I am not so wise, Solé, nor so foolish to imagine I know what hope is. But I know it is an act, not a thought."

"Do we have it?"

"I don't know. But I know we are still walking."

"You mean you are still walking. And Gundi."

Gundi was the name Solé had given to the mule when he was barely old enough to speak. In their language it meant cinnamon. Solé's mother had joked once that Gundi could stay in the house only if he smelled like cinnamon, which he most certainly did not.

"Gundi is old, but he is strong." Aldo smiled. "And

maybe I am the same."

"I can walk a bit, Papa. You can ride."

Aldo stopped and made his way back to the wagon and lifted Solé from the driver's seat. He felt his son's ribs under the linens.

"The road is not far," Aldo said. "But you must eat. Let's eat the loaves and raise our strength. We have a lot to do."

"I don't know, Papa. I don't feel good about this. Let's just go back."

Aldo nodded.

"It's all right to be afraid, my son."

"We got to be together for a while. Maybe that's enough. Maybe we're not supposed to go all the way there."

Aldo nodded and stroked the new growth of his beard. "Maybe."

"But you don't believe that, do you?"

"No, Solé. I don't believe that."

"So we're going to keep walking?"

"I'm afraid so, Solé. I don't think this journey is just for us."

"What do you mean?"

Aldo smiled tenderly. "Let me see how to explain it," he said, his eyes darkening as he stared into the distances before them. "I went fishing with my father often, when I was a boy. He was a strange man. He used to look down into the depths of the sea and say, 'The way down is the way up.' Then he would tap his chest and say, 'The way in is the way out.' I didn't understand his words until just now."

"Tell me what they mean, Papa."

Aldo turned back toward his son. "I will, Solé. Maybe tonight, under the stars."

"And then you'll tell me where we're going, and why?"

"If I discover that myself," Aldo smiled, "you will be the first to know."

They were sitting in the wagon, breaking the bread. Aldo took down a wineskin from where it hung on one of the wagon's ribs. He held it in his hands and looked at it, as though he were seeing something his son could not. Then he thumbed open the cork and lifted the wineskin to his lips.

"What does it taste like?" Solé asked.

Aldo thought for a long time.

"It tastes like the first night I met your mother."

Solé grimaced, and Aldo shook with laughter.

"I don't suppose you want to hear about that, then?"

"Can I taste it?"

Aldo handed the wineskin to his son and nodded. Solé tilted it back and took a tremendous swallow, as though he were drinking from the water flask. He gagged and spat out the wine on Gundi's haunches.

"It's like fire."

Aldo was laughing softly as he gathered back the wineskin and hung it up on the wagon-rib.

"Yes, Solé. There is a time for everything. This drink has brought many lives to ruin. Many Empires. Many kings. One day I will teach you how to drink it. But not now." Aldo's face had grown serious. "But do you see how I have taken only a little?"

"Yes."

"Good, Solé. Then you have already begun to learn."

Aldo lay back in the wagon, and Solé lay beside him and rested his head on his father's chest. He was thinking about what his father had said about listening to the hearts of others.

"I would let you into the gates of my life," Solé said, his voice already heavy with sleep, "if you were waiting outside."

When Solé woke, his father had pulled back the canvas of the wagon, revealing a clear sky with many stars.

"I've been thinking about what you asked," Aldo said, "about hope."

"So you'll give me a lesson on hope?"

"No, Solé. We might carry hope, but it is not something we learn at the beginning of a journey."

"Then what? What do we learn?"

"I think you know," Aldo said.

Solé lay back and looked up at the stars. He knew which lesson was coming.

Lesson 2: GRIEF

"Solé, I have told you about listening, and it is a lesson we must never forget. Tell me, then, what you felt when your mother died, and I will listen."

"I'm ashamed to say it," Solé whispered.

"There is no feeling for which you need to be ashamed."

"Really?"

"Yes. The moment we fear our own feelings is the moment we become strangers to ourselves. And those who are strangers to themselves are those who destroy worlds." Aldo ran a thumb across his son's lips, as though opening a seal. "Tell me."

"Papa, I felt nothing. I mean when it happened. When we were kneeling on either side of Mama and her breath came one last time, like a strange rattle, and you looked at me and said something about a story—at that moment I felt nothing at all."

"And you are ashamed of this?"

"Yes, of course. She never raised a hand to me or made me cry except when I deserved it. She stitched my clothes and made me a wool coat every winter. And she read to me. And she sang to me every night. I can still hear her voice."

Aldo heard his son's voice crack.

"You feel a great many things now, don't you?"

Solé nodded. He could not get himself to speak.

"Then you must not blame yourself for what you did not feel in the past. When something happens that is too vast for our lives, we may not feel it enter us."

"Like the horse of the Trojans?"

"Grief is different. We do not need to trust it to let it in."

"You mean we don't always know when it's in us?"

"Yes. I mean that."

"And what does it do once it's inside?"

"That is the hard part. It does its work. It begins

to change us before we even know we are being changed."

"I don't like it," Solé said.

"No one does, Solé. And we may only know many years later that it has been in us all awhile. It will show in our actions. In our words. We may look back at the shape our life has taken and say, 'Grief did that. Grief was shaping my life.'"

"I don't want that, Papa. I want to know what's shaping my life."

Aldo nodded. "Look at the stars," he said.

"I knew you'd say that, Papa. When you don't know what to say, you just say, 'Look at the stars.'"

Aldo smiled. "Well? What do you see?"

"I don't know. I don't know what the stars are."

"Neither do I," Aldo said. "I used to ask my father about them many times. He spent so many nights at sea, asking them to guide him. Then he told me a story I'll never forget."

"Can you tell it to me?"

Aldo smiled. "Of course, Solé."

Solé nuzzled close to his father.

"There was a man once," Aldo said, "whose work it was to interpret dreams. Not just any dreams, Solé, but the dreams of a king. The king would dream of mountains, and the man would say they meant his brothers. The king would dream of a river, and the man would say it meant his mother. But one morning the king woke and told the man of his dream. It was of the stars. All of them, bright and shining and so far away. 'What do they mean,' the king asked. The man thought for a very long time, and then he said, 'They are the stars, and they mean the stars.'"

Aldo looked at his son.

"Grief has taught me that, Solé. This world is mystery enough. Sometimes we just need to look. To see it for what it is. To be here."

They lay side by side for a long time. When Solé spoke again, his voice was quiet.

"I don't know about the stars, Papa. Maybe they're not just the stars. Mama used to say they're the dead, camped around their little fires, watching us from afar."

"Who can say? I like to think so, too."

"But you don't believe it?"

"What did I say about belief? You must believe what brings you peace. Others will say such beliefs are foolish. But I say each life has more wisdom than it can imagine. When your body thirsts, you drink. When your body aches for salt, you eat salt. Why should we not believe a thing when that belief soothes our hearts? How do we know the heart is not as much a guide as the mind?"

"Then I'll tell you what I think," Solé said. "I think Mama is up there, crouched by a little fire, making bread again. And I think she'll be waiting for me. And I think she'll hand me a small glass of water, a little piece of lemon in the dark."

"That is a marvelous story."

Solé rolled his head onto his father's chest again. "Papa, what were you saying about stories when Mama died? You looked at me across her bed and you said something to me about stories. Do you remember?"

"I do."

"Can you tell me?"

Aldo sat up in the wagon and cradled his son in his arms. He took Solé's hand and laid it on his heart. "I said her story is not over, Solé. This is where her story is now."

They found the road the next morning, and by noon they were in the city of Boacea. Solé's eyes widened, and he closed them tightly and opened them again.

"This is quite the oasis," he laughed.

The buildings were bright blue, with awnings of red and gold, and the children who ran in the streets were not thin. He turned to his father and asked if this is where they would stay.

"For tonight, yes."

The fluttering in Solé's stomach withered at the thought of their visit being so brief. He leapt down from the wagon and walked beside his father, holding his hand.

"Will we show them what we've made?"

Solé looked back toward the wagon, which carried

the arrows and bows they'd fashioned in the workshop. When they'd made them, he'd asked his father what they were for, but Aldo had only told him there are objects in life we cannot understand when they are apart from their use. "The heart," he said, "is like that. You cannot know it until you use it." He'd lifted an arrow and smoothed its eagle feathers that Solé had gathered in the foothills. Then he'd closed one eye and peered down its length. "These things are such things."

They were walking now down the streets of Boacea, and Solé could smell fresh bread in the air. He thought of the things people can make. Some make bread. Some make kingdoms. But he and his father had made the things that were in the wagon.

"Will we show them?" Solé asked again.

"Not yet," Aldo said, almost in a whisper. "Not here."

From the tone of his father's voice, Solé knew not to ask again. He turned his eyes back to the brilliant blue buildings, the intricate awnings, the merchants' stalls brimming with fresh fruit.

"Do we have enough money to eat?"

"I'll take care of that, Solé. You wait here."

He helped Solé back onto the driver's seat and pulled the mule and wagon into the shade of an alley. Then he walked to the back of the wagon and pulled something from a bundle and raised it up. It was a toy horse, one of the figures Solé loved.

"You'll sell it?"

Aldo winked at Solé and gestured for him to lie down in the wagon and rest.

"I'll be back," he said.

He returned with four fresh loaves of bread, six oranges, and a long piece of dried, salted meat. He'd filled the water flask that was slung over his shoulder, and he'd tied two more flasks to its lanyard.

"The merchant's son loves horses," he said. "Perhaps luck truly is on our side."

When they'd eaten their fill, they tucked away what was left and washed their hands with the smallest amount of water.

"We are in a wonderful place," Aldo said. They could hear music not far away. "We can't forget the soul needs nourishment, too."

He climbed out of the wagon and let Solé ride on

his back, as they'd done years ago. They crossed the street and pushed open a large, red door in one of the shimmering blue walls. No one turned to look at them, so raucous was the crowd inside. There were people drinking from large, tin cups; half-clothed figures dancing on the tables; musicians drawing music from their instruments, as one might draw up a writhing net of fish from the sea.

Aldo backed out of the door and let Solé slide down to stand beside him. "Your mother would not have liked a place like that," he said.

Down the street they came to another door, and Solé laid his ear against it. "I'm listening," he said. Aldo mussed his son's hair and knocked twice and waited.

They sat at a small table, which they shared with an elderly man and a young woman. A child played a zither in the corner, and the music filled the room with a gentleness that felt, to Aldo, like the hands of his late wife, Mara. Each night since her death he had spoken her name aloud, when he asked for her safe passage to wherever she was going, and he said it under his breath now as the music played. Mara. Mara.

The old man was called Pari, and he told his new

acquaintances that his name meant wanderer, though they had never heard such a name as that.

"This," the old man had said, "is my granddaughter. You may call her Gemma."

No doubt the woman was beautiful, but Solé felt only a vague ache he did not understand, and to Aldo, every woman was a sister to his wife, someone who could bring her memory back for a brief while, but whom he would never touch.

"We are from the South," Gemma said, and then, tapping her grandfather's shoulder, "Eat, tata. We have a long way to go."

"Where are you going?" Solé asked.

Aldo laid his hand gently on his son's hand.

"It's okay," the old man said to his granddaughter, "you can tell them."

Gemma looked once over her shoulder, and seeing only the child with the zither she leaned forward and spoke.

"You haven't heard, then, what's happening in Asha?"

Solé looked into his father's eyes for an answer.

No one spoke.

Finally the old man laid his crust of bread on the table and sighed. "I have lived eighty-seven years. Eighty-

45

seven. And I have always preached, to anyone who would listen, and most of all to myself, a life of peace. There is only one reason," he said, "to pick up a weapon."

Gemma was shaking her head. "I'd thought we were done with the time of tyrants. But the world will never learn. A people hand their lives into the hands of a tyrant, for what reason? So they don't have to carry those lives. So they don't have to carry their own questions."

The old man nodded, as though he had heard all this before. "Yes," he said, "Very few can carry their own lives."

Solé was squinting, trying to understand. He thought of the words his father had said in the desert. He looked up at his father, but Aldo said nothing.

"Asha," the old man said to Solé. "Do you know where that is?"

Solé looked at his father.

"I know it's a great city in the West. Papa has told me about it. I know the people look different from us there."

Aldo looked at his son. "That is not something I said to you. What makes you say they look different?"

"I've read about it, Papa," Solé said. "Even the old books say this."

"And this is the first thing you remember about Asha?"

Solé lowered his head at his father's words.

"I'm sorry," he said. "Please tell me about Asha. I'll listen."

Gemma smiled. "This is a most polite young man." Her smile drained away from her face. "But I'm afraid what we tell you is not very polite. It will no doubt be difficult for any of us to be polite in such a world."

Aldo lifted a hand for the proprietor. He handed him two silver coins, then gestured toward the old man and Gemma and handed him two more.

"You needn't do that," the old man said.

"I know. But I've done it. And now we must be going."

"So soon?"

"Yes. I'm sorry."

The old man seemed briefly hurt by this abruptness, but then his face softened. "I understand," he said, reaching over to tap Solé on both shoulders. "Go, and may peace be with you."

Solé and Aldo were walking back to the wagon in silence. Finally Solé spoke.

"So that's where we're going?"

Aldo reached for his son's hand, and they held each other without a word as they made their way to the wagon in the shadows.

They were back on the road by mid-afternoon, and the sun was much abated by a bank of clouds that had come in from the East.

"Perhaps it will rain," Aldo said. "We must be ready."

He hobbled the mule and took out two tin basins from the wagon and lashed them to the driver's seat, out of the cover of the canvas.

"The road is smooth," he said. "What rain we gather, we will keep."

Solé sat between the tin basins and watched the withers of the mule rise and fall. He had fed him two crusts of bread and an orange, but he saw the animal's ribs were as sharp as his own and his father's.

"How old is Gundi?" he asked.

"How many years have we had him?"

"Eleven. As long as I've been alive."

"Then—" Aldo scratched the growth of his beard, which he'd shaved before their journey, and which had always grown quickly. It was not as dark as it once had been. "Then he is over forty years old. The man I bought him from said he had lived through twenty winters, but I bought him in Divara, and to the numbers of the mule-traders of Divara, you must always add ten."

"Forty," Solé wondered. "That's about four Solés."

His father laughed and patted Gundi's haunches. He knew what question was next to come.

"How old are you, father?"

"Do you not know?"

"I forget. Time seems like such a dream since Mama died."

This thought moved Aldo to deep contemplation. My son is the greatest pupil I could have asked for, he said to his own heart. No doubt he will one day be my teacher.

"My child," he said, "I am one and a half Gundis."

They slept that night under the palm trees by a small pond just off the road. The desert had given way to grassland, and in the low-lying plains the rare rainwater stayed for weeks or more, held by the hard-baked earth beneath the roots of the grass.

They'd covered the wagon with the canvas again, and late in the night a rain began to fall. It woke them both.

"What's a tyrant, Papa?"

Aldo tapped his own heart in the darkness. "This."

"What?"

"Nothing, my child. Just a joke."

"A tyrant is a joke?"

Aldo thought about it. "Well, yes, in a way. But a cruel joke. A joke that must be told to the whole world, so people hear it."

"Hear what?"

"Hear what is happening."

"Papa." Solé's voice rose in passion. "How am I supposed to know what's happening if you never tell me clearly?"

At this he heard his father breathe a deep sigh.

"I knew this moment would come."

"Good," Solé said. He smiled and lowered his voice to sound, as much as he could, like his father. "Very good."

Lesson 3: POWER

You've asked me what a tyrant is. This is a difficult word.

Let me say it this way, Solé. I am glad we had company today. You must always remember that a life must have its solitude, but to cultivate your loneliness out of fear is an error. Many people spend their nights alone, weeping because no one hears them. And then a stranger appears at the door, and they send him away.

Our lives are fragments. "No one," we say, "can understand the pieces of my heart." And yet we fall in love with our brokenness. We forget we must take the great risk.

We must try to be a story.

    This is a great mystery, my child. For there are times in life when we can hold someone and feel the truth of their life, behind any story that is told of them, any story they tell of themselves. And they feel the same in us. But those are the rarest moments of all, my child. Those are the moments of grace. Those are the moments of love. And a tyrant is only someone who is powerless, powerless to feel that.

    What you heard today in Boacea was not wrong. A person can become so afraid of his own life that he asks someone else to carry it. This is what a tyrant does. He makes you afraid of yourself. He tells you there is something dark and vicious in the world, some enemy always at your gates, and you do not even know that he is describing your own shadow. He may call this shadow by different names: them, those people, the enemy. But all the while he is talking about you. And because you are so afraid, because you cannot carry that fear, you ask the other to carry it for you, and you make war against that other, and you seek to destroy them. But all the while you are destroying yourself.

I know you do not understand all that I say. Perhaps I do not understand either, my child. But I know this. When someone makes you fear yourself, they can make you do anything. They can make you do things you never dreamt you could do. They can make you silence even your own voice, even the voice in your heart.

And so it is with tyrants. They bind you with your own fears, and they tell you they are the freedom from those fears. And they lead you into slaughter, into destruction, into chains. Very often you cannot see those chains, Solé. Very often you cannot hear what that tyrant is saying, nor any true words at all, for the lies of a tyrant so infect the world that you forget the sound of truth.

This is the method of those who control you. They take away your freedoms and tell you it is to keep you safe. They lull your spirit into sleep, deep sleep, and the imprisonment lasts for as long as you comply. And then, on your death bed, old as you have become, you open your eyes and see what you have done. You turn to the one beside you, if there is anyone left, and you say to her, "Tell me I lived my life." And she cannot.

Always remember this: anyone can be a tyrant. You

do not need a crown. All you need is the fault of believing that the ways in which you have been wronged give you a right to rule others. For then vice is done in the name of virtue. And then anyone who touches your life will meet terror. And then others will come to suffer, even in the small acts of your ignorance. They will see why the flag of those who do not know themselves is always the most powerful in the world.

So it goes, my son. It is our nature to tire of carrying our lives. But it takes strength, true strength, not to lay your life in the wrong hands, as though that surrender would be rest. There is only one who can carry us and leave us who we are, dance us and give us rest, give our lives a shape and make us free.

And you will learn in time who that is.

Solé had fallen asleep, and he was dreaming. He dreamt of his mother walking beside the wagon with them, singing. Always she had sung to him in the nights, and her songs were sweet and deep and true, and he never knew if she had made them up or had heard them somewhere long ago.

He was dreaming of the last song she had sung to him, before her illness had taken her voice away.

My Light, your eyes are honey sweet.
Your shadow's wings are furled.
Come, my Light, your breath can be
The beginning of the world.

When he woke, his eyes were wet. He had not known you can cry in your sleep, but he knew he was on a great journey, and if he reached its end, he would have learned a great many things. "There are things in life we cannot understand when they are apart from their use," his father had told him, and Solé lay awake now and thought about that. He thought perhaps his father was saying there are things we cannot learn until we live them. And that this is why many people do not live their lives.

The days had grown very hot, and they traveled now only in the late afternoons and the early evenings. At times Solé walked with his father, but his father always lifted him again and placed him in the driver's seat, or in the back of the wagon. Sometimes his father would sing.

"Why are you always so quiet," Aldo asked, "when I am singing? It would be a lot less lonesome if you sang with me."

At this, the wagon grew silent. Aldo squinted and leaned toward it as he walked.

"Solé?"

"Papa," the boy answered. "Can I tell you something, and you'll promise not to be upset?"

"Of course."

Solé was silent for a moment more. Then he said, "You do not sing as well as Mama."

Aldo's heart rose, and he burst into laughter.

"No," he said, "no, I most certainly do not."

That afternoon Solé was asleep when the wagon jolted. He woke to see his father struggling with the spokes of a wheel, tilting his head as he considered them.

"They'll hold," he said. "They have to."

"Papa?"

Solé was peeking out of the wagon's canvas.

"What's the matter, Papa?"

"Nothing."

"Don't say nothing. Something's wrong."

Aldo wiped his hands on his thighs.

"You're right. I'm just not sure about the sand. It gets in the flange and stresses the spokes against the felloes."

"You don't have to use big words. You could explain it so I can understand." He paused. "Mama would have."

Aldo moved his lips as if to answer, but Solé had already vanished into the wagon again.

"Mama would have," he said again, from within.

When night fell, the axle broke again. They repeated the work they'd done a few days earlier, and when it did not hold, Aldo kicked at the axle and swore.

Solé squinted at his father.

"I'm sorry," Aldo said. "How foolish it is to be angry at a wagon. It is only a thing. And look how far it has carried us."

"I don't mind, Papa. Can I tell you something else?"

"Of course." Aldo was rubbing his toe in its leather boot.

"Sometimes it's nice to hear you make a mistake."

Aldo's laugh filled the air, and it seemed it would wake the citizens of Boacea, which was now a two days' walk away.

They had fixed the axle again with a third rib of the wagon, and the canvas hung down nearly to their faces when they lay back to rest.

"Already it is you who are teaching me," Aldo said.

"I don't know," Solé sighed. "I don't feel I know anything at all."

"You must never lose that feeling."

They were quiet awhile before Solé spoke. His voice was soft and clear in the stillness of the night.

"Papa?"

"Yes."

"Can we talk about mistakes?"

Aldo sighed, brushing the sand from his eyes.

"On that subject," he said, "I have much to tell."

Lesson 4: MISTAKES

From what I have said to you, Solé, perhaps you have the impression that I have lived a perfect life. You know in your heart this isn't so. And if I leave you with this feeling that I have not transgressed, then I have made the greatest transgression of all.

I kicked the wagon today. Perhaps we're always most angry at that which has carried us. You must think more, one day, about what carries you. I have told you that tyrants carry us, and they keep us from ourselves. But love is a different thing. Love can carry us, too. Only it does not keep us from ourselves. Love is not a shelter from ourselves.

Perhaps I am saying too much at once. Let me slow down. I kicked the wagon today. That was a foolish thing to do, but a human thing. Your mother would have told me that: how foolish to be human, she used to say, and how much more foolish not to be. But your mother was wiser than I am, Solé, in more ways than I can tell.

What I am trying to tell you—I have avoided it this far in our journey—is that there are two kinds of people: those who want to be perfect, and those who want to be whole. You must strive, Solé, to be one of the latter. For those who want to be perfect are those who do the worst harm of all.

Remember those palm trees growing by the side of the road? How wonderful they were, with their shadows. Those shadows gave us such rest, while the sun gave us pain. Sometimes it is the other way around. But we need both on our journey, and we carry both in ourselves.

How often we go in fear of our shadows. But what if we loved that part of us, Solé? What if we saw the darkness in us and spoke with it, invited it to our tables, asked it what it wanted? I have spoken to you about tyrants, Solé. Now perhaps you are ready to see: if you deny your shadow, it becomes your tyrant. If you deny your shadow, you find it everywhere in the world.

Like those palm trees, waving in the breeze: what has no shadow, a great poet said once, has no strength to live. That is a wonderful sentence, and I have thought about it often. When you were born, I held you in that little barn, and the moon shone through the planks of the roof, and I saw your little shadow wriggling on the floor. I will love that too, I said to myself, and I will teach him to love it also.

I hope that I have done that for you, Solé. For we will come, soon, to our destination. And we do not yet know what will be asked of us when we arrive. And perhaps we will have to have become very good at forgiving ourselves, very good indeed.

I could tell you of my mistakes in this life, Solé, and perhaps one day I will. But I must choose wisely. For there is a difference between our children and our friends, and I must not confuse the two. What I do, and what I have done, has the power to shape your life. And the difference between a good heart and a wicked one is what it does with its power.

I can sense in your heart that you are lonely at times on this journey. I know the time will come when I cannot give you the company you need. And then you will have to carry your loneliness. And that is a great trial. It can bring us to many wrong doors. It can try to tell us so many lies are our home.

Remember the orchids in our garden back home, blooming in the April sun? Once, when you found me sitting alone with those little gifts—do you remember?—you asked me what I was thinking. I can tell you now. I was thinking that so many lives squander their loneliness. I was thinking that we must use our pain for the great thing it wishes to do. I was thinking every blossom says to us, in its language of silences, *What have you done with your dark time?*

Solitude is a blessing, my son, but a long road of loneliness stretches before it. And loneliness is a great mystery. Who among us does not fear being alone? But I tell you, Solé, so many of my mistakes have come from my loneliness. For when we panic in our loneliness, we reach for a companion, even the wrong companion, and we hurt even the ones we think we've come to love. For even love can be a betrayal, if we love each other for what we are not.

I will keep learning until the day something closes the little book of my heart. I will keep reading its mysteries if I can. Perhaps I have learned very little of what is written there. But I know some of it. I know we are afraid if we heal ourselves no one will know us at all. I know this, my son: In the silence of my darkest night, I asked the world, *Why, why I have been afraid to heal my life?*

And the answer came: *Because you are afraid to be alone.*

I grow tired, Solé. It is not easy to speak of one's mistakes. But for you I do it. For you I would walk into any fire.

For above all, I have learned, I must be honest with myself about what I have done. If I am not, there will be a terrible silence in my life, and then there will be a terrible silence in yours. And in the terrible silences of our lives, the worst stories can grow.

Do you hear those wolves in the distance? They do not have anger in their hearts, or vengeance, or forgiveness.

But we do, while we live. And we must choose which feeling will lead our lives. We must choose, my son, because each life has the great task to waken. And to waken yourself is to save a stranger's world.

I could speak forever, Solé. Perhaps it soothes me on our journey. Perhaps it soothes you. But remember that all the words in the world cannot replace the silence. And the touch of love. And those little words your mother taught you so long ago.

You know what they are, don't you?

Say them, and feel your life grow. Because a life that says I am sorry is a life that has grown.

And those small words are most powerful when you say them with your life, Solé, with your life.

I can speak of mistakes only because I have lived so long. In time, we all lose the path. And then we find ourselves alone with guilt. For what is guilt except the feeling of being cast out from our home?

But you must carry your guilt only as long as it takes to wake you, Solé, and then you must set it down. Love does not want us to suffer, but only to change, only to waken. You must be there for the ones who need you. And you can only do that if you set the old ghosts down.

Let me tell you a little story. Perhaps I have told it before.

Once, your mother and I had argued over something small. It was so small we had forgotten what it was. But we were still angry with one another. We carried ourselves through the rooms of our small home in silence. We bumped against each other and said nothing. We slept curled away from each other in the dark.

Do you know who brought us out of that darkness, Solé? You did. You could not have been more than five. But you were always you, my son. You climbed into bed with us, and took your mother's hand, and took my hand, and you wrapped them together with the belt of your mother's tunic. "Now," you said, tapping my chest, and then tapping your mother's, "when you hurt you hurt."

I do not know what I have done to deserve you, Solé, but I shall try to teach you what I can, because it has been clear to me from the beginning that you are one with a chance to do something astonishing. And that is all. The chance is all.

Come, then, let us proceed on our journey of

mistakes. Let us sing to ourselves a small song, which your mother would have sung:

> *Regret, regret*
> *Just long enough to change.*
> *To live is to awaken.*
> *To live is to forgive.*

At times, when they rested, Solé looked out over the grasslands and saw foothills, a blue line of mountains in the distance. He could see large holes in the hills, and he asked his father what they were.

"Caves."

"Are there wolves there?" Wolves had begun to roam through his mind since his father had spoken of them. He had heard about the great packs of them in the stories his mother had told.

"Something like that," his father answered.

"What does that mean?"

Aldo smiled. "Don't worry, Solé." He tapped his chest. "Remember there are wolves in here, too. Do what you can to understand them. The rest we cannot worry over."

"Then why are we bringing these arrows to Asha?"

Aldo lifted his chin and looked at his son. "There is nothing you do not see, is there?"

Solé was not sure if this was a good thing, and he lowered his head. But his father touched his chin and lifted it.

"That is good, Solé. You're right. We are bringing these things we have made to Asha so that we can help the people there. There are indeed wolves in this world, and men can be the worst kind of wolf. There is a time to fight, yes, but first you must make sure you know whom you are fighting. First you must make sure you are not the wolf." He stroked Solé's face. "Do you understand?"

"I think so. Yes."

"Good," Aldo said, "because sometimes I am afraid I do not."

The next morning they lay side by side as a dust storm whistled through the canvas.

"Papa?"

"Yes?"

"I'm sorry I said Mama would have done better. When you were talking about the axle."

"That's okay, Solé. You're right. She would have."

"But it wasn't a nice thing to say."

"I suppose not."

"I'm sorry, Papa."

"It's quite all right. We're on a strange journey."

"Very."

Aldo turned toward his son and stroked his face.

"You're sorry?"

"Yes."

"Then you don't have to carry it anymore."

Their food was nearly gone, so they traveled again both night and day. On the seventh day of their journey, they had eaten everything they had traded for in Boacea. They had drunk the water they had gathered in the tin basins and transferred into the flasks, and they had begun to sip from the wineskin.

"It makes my head swim, Papa."

"I know, Solé. You must not drink it. Just wet your lips. Just tell your body you have not abandoned it."

They came to Zuzanna in the middle of the eighth day. Such a city Solé had never seen, and Aldo turned to him and said he, too, had never been to such a place.

He had only heard about it in books, in stories. For the buildings were raised on tall, wooden legs, like skittish cats trying not to touch the ground as they walked.

"Why do they build them that way, Papa?"

"Did you feel," Aldo asked, "how we rode down from the grasslands just now? It was slight but it was quite a long way down. They have built this place in the valley, where they are safe from the winds and the raiders of the plains, but when the rains come, these streets must be rivers. Look over there."

Solé followed his father's finger. He saw a small boat lashed to the porch of a house.

"But it rained just a few days ago, up in the plains. Does that mean the water is on its way?"

"I don't think so. The children would all be inside if that were so. Their mothers know best."

Solé was quiet as they rode on. After a while he grabbed the sleeve of his father's tunic and said, "Papa. What do you mean about raiders in the grasslands?"

Aldo laid his arm around his son. "We're past all that, Solé. On the other side of Zuzanna are the broad plains, where there are no hills, and where there are no hills there are no caves for raiders."

"Wolves, you mean."

Aldo smiled.

"Raiders, Papa. Raiders! But what if they had come to us when we were in the grasslands? What would have happened?"

"Solé, you must breathe now. There will be times of joy and times of sorrow. Times of ecstasy and times of darkness. I do not know which one we are bound for. But I know we must go on. That's all. I know sometimes we must work to change our hearts, and to change the world, but sometimes the work is just to wait, and to continue. Remember that everything will pass, Solé, everything."

"But Papa, what would have happened?"

"I don't know."

"But—" Solé could hear his voice trembling. "But you were ready?"

"I was ready."

They rode into the city, down from the last of the grasslands and onto the cobbled streets. There was a smell of dogwood flowers in the air. Children came to pat the dust from Gundi and laugh at the wagon with its creaking axle and its sagging canvas.

"Always imagine," Aldo said to Solé, "that the

laughter of others is meant to lighten your burdens. If it helps you laugh at yourself, is your journey not lighter?"

When they'd hobbled Gundi in the shadows, Aldo checked on the bows and arrows in the wagon and took down the canvas and shrouded them.

He stared at the wagon a long time. Then he lifted the canvas and bit it and ripped it in three places. He picked up some dirt and rubbed it into the sun-bleached green of the fibers. When he was finished, the wagon was a most pathetic sight.

"No one will steal from us now, Solé. There is no one more ignored in this world than the poor."

They found the sign for a lodging house, and they climbed the rickety stairs to its porch and knocked on the door. They could hear footsteps inside, and Aldo turned to Solé and smiled.

"Your beard is back," Solé said.

"Do you like it?"

Solé seemed to be trying to remember something, something he had heard a long time ago. "As long as it's not a mask."

Aldo squinted and cocked his head back in the air.

"Who taught you to say that?"

"Mama," Solé said. "She said it to you all the time. Don't you remember?"

"And you were listening?"

"Yes. I was listening."

They slept that night in one bed in the lodging house. They'd eaten a dinner of lamb chops, rice, and black bread, and they'd soothed their throats with well-water freshened with lemon.

When Solé had reached for his fourth chop, Aldo patted his hand.

"Eat," he said, "but do not give the body what it can't handle. In the morning we'll trade with the merchants, and we'll have plenty to take with us."

"But I've never been this hungry, Papa. How much longer do we have to go?"

"Not long," Aldo said, though when he said it he realized that all journeys are long for a child.

"You know, Solé. I don't think we've spent this long together in all my days. I like it."

"I like it, too, Papa."

"Let's pretend this is what life is. This being on the road. We meet people, we look at the stars, we sing our songs poorly." A smile flashed across Aldo's face, then vanished. "We are always in a rush to arrive," he said, "and then when we get there, something in our hearts sinks. We go about like sleepwalkers, searching for the next journey."

He looked at his hands. Then he spoke again.

"You never met your grandfather, Solé. My father was a strange man, but I loved him. Perhaps I loved him because of his strangeness."

"What made him so strange?"

"Oh, he was the strangest thing a person can be. He was an artist."

"An artist?"

"He would not have said so himself. Many times he sat me on his knee and said, 'All souls are artists, Dodo. Some of us forget how to be.'"

"He called you Dodo," Solé said, "just like Mama."

"Yes," Aldo said, "he would have liked Mama very much."

Solé looked at his own hands and then at his father's. He closed his eyes for a moment and then opened them.

"I would have liked to meet him."

"I would have liked that too, Solé. I used to stay up nights and watch my father working. Much as you watched me in the workshop, in that life that seems already so long ago, so far away."

Aldo looked at his son's feet in their worn leather sandals.

"Your grandfather carved figures of wood. He was a fisherman, as you know, and he would gather driftwood from the edge of the sea, or from the waves during his journeys, and he would carry the wood home. My mother always laughed at him as he waddled up the road, bearing such burdens. This was a long time ago, but I can still see it: my father in his white cotton tunic, his hair stiff with the salt air, a load of driftwood over his shoulders."

Aldo sighed. "You never saw my homeland, Solé. This was before the Great War, about which I will tell you in time. Before your mother and I had to leave, with only the things we carried. Our land had been a place of peace, and my father could make his figures, and the land was prosperous, and people would buy them."

"What would he make?"

"Your grandfather could look at you just once"— Aldo brushed a hand over his son's face, "and then he could remake you from grains and knots of wood. It was astonishing." He sighed again. "I think he was in great pain when he worked. But I never saw him so sad as when he was finished, and before he had begun."

Solé yawned. He could not help himself.

"Sorry, Papa."

"I do drift from what I was saying, don't I?" Aldo said. "I was telling you about journeys, and here we are talking about my father."

"I like talking about him."

"Good, Solé. A person is lost, like a piece of that driftwood, when he does not have his roots. When he does not have a home." He shook his head. "You will see when we get to Asha. Many are without homes in this world. You have already seen it in the faces of those we have come across. Many are exiles—from themselves, from their families, from their homes."

"What can they do," Solé asked, "if they can't go back?"

"They can tell stories, Solé. Or they can do what my father did. They can work on that driftwood of their own hearts until the image of what they are is revealed. So the world can see it. For those who know their own beauty always have a home."

In the morning, they loaded the wagon with grapes, cheese, and flatbread. Aldo took a thread and needle from beneath the driver's seat and stitched the tears in the canvas, then covered what was left of the wagon's ribs.

"Your mother could have done it better," he said. "I still wonder why it is I and not she on this journey with you, Solé. Perhaps she would have taken a different way. Perhaps you would have a different destination."

"But that's not the way it is."

"You're right, Solé. That's not the way it is."

They were back on the road for half a day before Solé spoke again. They both rode in the driver's seat, and Aldo had said the axle would hold. "It has to now. And it will."

"How many arrows do we have left?" Solé asked. "You've traded twice."

"I don't think we should think about that."

"Please, Papa. We're on this journey together. And we haven't even brought any books. I lie awake at night and imagine things, just as you've taught me, but I want to be part of the story. I want to imagine what will happen in Asha."

"I don't think I want to imagine that."

"Please, Papa."

Aldo stopped the mule and climbed down from the driver's seat and went around the back of the wagon. For a brief moment, Solé had a terrible vision.

When his father returned, he patted Solé on the head and said, "Three hundred, more or less. And one hundred bows."

Solé's eyes had darkened, and his father held him and asked him if he was feeling ill. "Do you need to stop? We should find some shade."

"No, Papa. I just—"

"Tell me, Solé."

"I had a terrible thought, when you were gone just now."

"I wasn't gone. I was only—"

"I know. But it was terrible."

"What did you think, Solé? You can tell me."

Solé looked up into his father's eyes.

"I thought you weren't coming back."

Aldo gathered up his son and held him close and began to rock him, as Solé's mother would have done.

"Then I think it is time," he said, "that we talked about hope."

Lesson 5: HOPE

I am thinking about what you said, Solé. That we did not bring books. You must understand how much I love them, and perhaps that is why I left them at home, so that I would not be tempted to lose myself in them. So that I would always be with you.

But I see now I should have brought them for you. My only consolation is that perhaps, without those other stories to fill your head, you will let yours fill your heart.

And you will remember.

I am a carpenter, a simple craftsman, and I have learned you cannot remake the world. Not all at once. But you can make changes. And although they may seem small, they are not. Like my father working on his figures. Like your mother working on your heart. Person by person, lesson by lesson, act by act. When you change a heart—especially if it is your own, my child—you have a chance, just a chance, to change the world.

You ask me what hope is. You asked at the beginning of our journey. I did not know I was going to say it, but I said then that hope is an action. It is something we do. And I believe that is true.

I have not told you about my darkest days. I thought perhaps I would always keep them from you. In time I will tell you about those days, and especially those nights. For the nights were the hardest. I will tell you how lonesome it was in my prison cell, when the Great War raged. I had spoken up against it, and I was thrown into the dungeon. That is one of the great questions, Solé: when do we act, and when to we let things be? I do not often know the answer, Solé, but I know it is a question injustice asks, and I know it is a question that love asks, and I know it is a question that hope asks, too.

I thought I would not survive those nights. I thought perhaps I would never become your father. Every night I heard prisoners being taken out of their cells and marched up to the courtyard, where terrible things were done to them. I will not tell you about those things. Not because I want to shield you from the world, but because you will know the world soon enough. And a child must have time to be a child. That is the greatest crime of all, Solé: to rob a child of his childhood, to take from him the magic and the awe. For each of us has a childhood that has never been before, and will never be again. And maybe those who cannot hope are those whose childhoods have been taken away. What reason would a life have to hope if its childhood had been taken? And that, Solé, that is why we are going to Asha.

So we go on. For us, this journey has been easy. But we never know when despair will come, like raiders on the road in their dark hoods, the hooves of their horses pounding like rain.

And when that happens, we may break. We may say that we are in despair, but then—look, just look: we see our hands still working, still fixing an axle, still brushing our child's hair as the thieves of life circle on their horses.

That is hope, I think: not a word, not even a promise we make to ourselves. It is the thing in us that will not easily be conquered. It is the eyes opening by morning, the left foot in front of the right, the heart still choosing to say beauty.

The human heart is the only thing in this universe that can open again while knowing why it closed.

On the twelfth day of their journey, the road began to climb. The mountains, which had for many days been a blue line in the distance, then a rising wave, now obscured the sky before them. They could see snow on the peaks.

"I don't know if Gundi can do it," Solé said. He climbed down and held the face of his mule, with whom he had shared his whole life. "Poor Gundi," he said. "We get to ride, and he has walked this whole way."

"A mule," his father said, "would be quite confused if someone put him in a wagon."

Solé did not smile. "Still," he said, "it's such a long way."

He went to the wagon and returned with grapes and held them up to Gundi, who lapped them up with his big, leathery lips, stems and all. He crouched down and nudged Gundi with his shoulder until the hooves came up, one at a time.

"He's not sore," he told his father. "But the mountains are so high."

"We'll take the pass, Solé. And then on the other side is Asha."

Solé looked up at where the sky cleaved the mountains.

"It's strange, Papa. All this time Asha seemed so unreal. Like a dream. Now that we're so close, I'm afraid."

"I am too, Solé. But this is when Gundi is the lucky one."

"You don't think he can be afraid?"

"Certainly he can. But he does not fear what we fear. Maybe in that way he gets to rest."

Solé patted Gundi's face and stroked his long ears. He leaned forward and sniffed his mane. "Old linens," his mother had said, "he smells like sour linens. But I love him because you do."

The sun was high in the mountains, and Aldo felt a chill in his heart when he thought they might not make it through before nightfall. The pass is dangerous, the maps had told him, when he'd studied them before their journey. Then he remembered that this was the night of the full moon, and even if they lost the sun, they would have that.

You see, he said to himself, I have been telling my child about hope, and all this time we have been walking. Among the raiders, among the rains, among hunger. And the moon has never abandoned us. The light has never left us. Step by step, he thought, ache by ache, walk your life toward hope.

There was no snow in the pass. When the sun fell, they were halfway through. By the light of the moon they could see the way, and they could see the faint lights of Asha in the distance.

"Is that it, Papa?"

"Yes."

"You sound tired."

"I am, Solé."

They drove on for a while, and though the sky creaked like an old dam, it did not break open.

By morning they had come down from the pass, and Solé was shivering. They could see the city down in the valley below. Aldo lifted his son and carried him to the back of the wagon and laid him down. Then he took down the canvas to reveal the sun.

"You must warm yourself, Solé, before we go on."

He lifted one of the water flasks they'd filled in Zuzanna and propped up his son and helped him drink.

"Are you hungry?"

"There's only one flatbread left, Papa. You have it."

Aldo shook his head.

"Don't be a hero, Solé. There will be time for that yet."

"I don't like when you say such things."

"I'm sorry, Solé. You're right. This is a very serious thing, and I shouldn't joke. But it's an old habit from long ago. Your grandfather always had a joke ready, even in the darkest times. Especially in the darkest times."

"I like when you joke, Papa. That's not what I meant."

"You meant Asha, then," Aldo, said, "that I should not speak about it?"

Solé yawned. "I don't know," he said, "what I meant. I'm tired, Papa. You can talk about whatever you want."

"No," Aldo said, "I can't. Not to you. That is how we are different."

"How?"

"There are things I cannot say to you, for you do not need to hear them. But you must be able to say to me anything you wish. Anything." His eyes were closed. "And if not to me, you must be able to say it to yourself."

He looked back at the pass in the mountains, then up at the snow-peaked cliffs, then at the valley where Asha lay.

"And Solé, if you cannot do that," he said, "then I have failed."

They lay beside each other in the sunlight. Solé slept as a child sleeps, with a great peace on his face. Aldo thought about what his son had said: "You look tired, Papa." He felt his tiredness now. For weeks he had held it off, but now it came flooding into him, like water through the streets of Zuzanna, and he could not hold his head above it. He curled beside his son in the wagon and felt the bows and arrows against his back, and he tried not to think of the next part of their journey, and very soon he too was asleep, the day's sweat drying in his tunic, a scent of oil in his hair.

For days he had doubted the purpose of their

journey, but in his sleep he dreamt of a great book lying in the streets of an abandoned city. In his dream he lifted the book and opened it and blew the dust from the pages. It was full of names.

He began to say them aloud—quickly, at first, and then slowly. There were so many, and he let their sounds roll over his tongue, until he was almost singing. He thought about what Solé had said about his songs. He tried to remember how he had answered. We must sing our song, he thought, even if we sing it poorly. In his dream, he let the book fall into the dust of the street, and he looked around him. No one was there. Then, in the shadow of a doorway, he saw a tall, dark figure. He squinted, and the figure stepped forward into the light.

"Father," he said, "what's happened here?"

"Don't you know?"

"No. Teach me."

"This is the city you did not reach in time. This is the city that was destroyed." He waved his hand in a strange gesture. "They are all gone."

In his dream, Aldo looked down at the book at his feet. "And these names?"

"You know what they are."

Aldo could feel the tears welling in his eyes.

"Do not cry, Dodo. There is still one thing you can do."

Aldo looked up. His father had lifted a piece of driftwood in his arms, and he was cradling it as a mother would cradle a child.

"What, father? What can I do?"

His father stepped back into the shadows.

"One thing," his father said again. "One thing."

Aldo woke with a start and turned to see Solé sleeping. Very gently he roused him.

"Come," he said. "We have little time."

"I'm not ready, Papa."

"I know. Nor am I."

"My skin itches," Solé said. "We haven't bathed in so long."

Aldo looked back toward the mountain. "We should have done that earlier. Now there is nowhere to do it. You're right, Solé, we should be clean before we get to Asha."

He searched through the wagon, among the bundles, and lifted the last full flask and opened it.

"Come," he said. "Quickly."

They stood outside the wagon and stripped naked and washed themselves. The water was cool, and the air slid down from the mountain and raised goosebumps on their bodies. They dressed quickly and climbed up into the wagon again and held each other close.

"Solé," Aldo said. "Remember that we did that so as to be fresh for our hosts."

"I know."

"Remember the flesh must be tended to, but when I say we must be clean I do not mean there is any stain in your soul." He looked at his son. "There is nothing within you that is dirty."

Solé nodded and then laid his head on his father's shoulder.

"Can you tell me another lesson? It would help me."

"We must talk as we move, then."

"All right. Just talk to me."

"I will, my son. I will."

Lesson 6: Courage

The time will come, very soon, Solé, when you will have to be the one who does the teaching. I can feel it. But you have asked me to talk to you, and I know that soothes you, so I will.

I do not know what waits for us in Asha. I know only what the whispers have been throughout the land. Perhaps by the time we arrive, it will all be over. It seems already many days ago that we spoke to Gemma and the old man. And it was many days before that when a strange visitor came to me at home, speaking of Asha, asking me to take this journey.

No doubt he asked many throughout the land, for I am only a humble craftsman, and why should my creations be any better than anyone else's? But then I remembered what my father told me: you never know, Dodo, when fate is knocking at your door. You never know when you are talking to your life.

I can hardly tell you if I believe in such things, Solé. But I believe this is a journey I had to make. Perhaps I shouldn't have brought you. Perhaps I am only walking you into a den of lions. What kind of father am I?

But then I think of you at home, so far away, and I think of all the things I would not have had time to tell you. And then my heart aches as it has only ached once before in this life.

You have said to me that you are afraid. And I have told you I am. There is a story I have never told you, Solé, about a man on his deathbed. His son came to him after a long journey, and the man was elated that his son had come.

"Father," the son said, "I am afraid."

"For you or for me, Aldo?" For the son in the story was I.

"I am afraid for both of us."

The man raised a hand and brought his son to his chest and embraced him. His son was a man now, and he had last seen him when he was very young.

"You're strong, Aldo. You must not let that hurt you."

The son stood up and squinted at his father.

"Why would my strength hurt me, father? I don't understand."

The man, who was very old, closed his eyes. When he opened them again, they were moist with tears.

"How can we know what to do in this life?" he said. "There is much against which we must fight. We must defy. We must hold out. For I believe the creators survive the destroyers. I do believe that."

"It's time to rest now, father. You're very weak."

"Create something, Aldo," the old man said. "No matter what it is. Create."

The son did not know what to say, but he stayed by his father's side. After a long while the old man spoke again.

"It's late," he said, "where is your mother?"

The son shook his head. He had not known his father's memory was so bad, so near the end.

"She died long ago, father. In our house by the sea."

"Ah, yes," the old man said, as though he were remembering something that had long ago ceased to touch his heart.

"She could have said it better. But this is who I am. I am a man, a very old man, and I can only teach you as the person I am. If I had pretended to be something else, all my teaching would have been in vain."

"I know, father. But what are you teaching me? We haven't seen each other in so long."

The man reached out his hand, and his son took it.

"Aldo," he said, "what does your name mean?"

"It means wise."

"Yes. Perhaps it was a foolish name to give you. There are no wise men in this world. Only apprentices. Only messengers."

"I don't understand, father." The son had the feeling that his father was drifting away, saying things that made little sense.

Then the old man's eyes sparkled with light.

"Messengers," he said, "and each of us is carrying the message."

"What message, father?" The son was ashamed of his impatience with a dying man.

"The message we are all carrying."

"You're scaring me, father. Please. I'm afraid."

The old man held his son's sleeve and pulled him down again and embraced him.

"That is the message," he said. "We all are."

The young man stood up again and watched his father close his eyes.

"Rest, father. Let's not talk like this. Let's talk about the old days."

"The old days." The man's eyes were open now, and they were very far away.

"The sea," the son said, "and our little house by the stream."

"I remember."

There was a silence between them. Neither spoke until the old man lifted his hand to his son's face.

"I feel an anger in you, Aldo. Let me tell you this one thing. I remember my father. I remember his anger. I remember he had nowhere to set it down. Every family, my son, has a great anger in it. Or a great sorrow. Or a great fear. But it does not mean you have to carry it in your own heart forever. You do not have to carry the heart of a ghost. All you have to do is feel it once. Truly feel it."

The man had cradled his son's face again.

"In our lives, Aldo," the old man said, "inside our

lives is where the dead can change."

The son laid his hand on his father's forehead. It was very cold.

"Now it's really time to rest, Papa. No more of this."

The old man's hands were trembling.

"You have not yet fought your battles," he said, "but they are coming. Perhaps they will be with others. Perhaps they will be with yourself."

"I have had my share of battles."

"Do not be proud, my son." The words were barely a whisper. "Open your heart and listen."

The son felt his heart close. This man had not seen him in so long, and now he was daring to teach him. But something in him made him lean toward his father and listen.

"You already know," the old man said, "that courage is not the absence of fear. So I will not teach you that."

The son felt his father's cold hand on his back. It was like a strange bird that had fallen to earth, after crossing the tremendous distances of the sea.

"I wish," the old man said, "that I had known this long ago. But now I can tell you. The hardest thing to carry is a fear without a name. We may find a name for it, but so many lives are lost in the effort to find the name of their fear. In their haste to escape it, they give that fear the wrong name. They say they are afraid of something, of someone, when that something is only a vessel to hold their fear. We do this with our hatred, too. We do this with our wounds. We give them a name, and a face, and we say we are courageous for facing those faces. But all the while we are fighting the wrong battle."

His breath was ragged, but he spoke on.

"And when we fight the wrong battles, we suffer more when they are over. For we have done harm. And we are cast back to the wound in us that has no name. This is why many do not wish their battles to end. This is why many make war without cease."

The son knelt beside his father. His heart was open, and he told himself to remember his father's words, every one of them. He told himself this is why he had come this long way.

The old man's voice was very weak from having spoken for so long. But he touched his son's face and nodded.

"I have one more thing to tell you, my son."

"Please, father. Yes."

"It is that way with love, too. Every life is a ghost story. We put those ghosts into the ones we think we love.

We give them those masks. And then, one day, it happens: the ghosts go from those faces, and we must see the truth standing before us. That is the question that courage asks. Real courage. What will you do when the ghosts go? What will you do when you see who is standing before you?"

The man closed his eyes and let out his breath, and his son held him a long time in the moonlight, and he told himself one day he would understand his father's words. One day he would understand his father's hands, those old hands torn by the years, like the deep-grooved gloves a falconer, who has learned the infinite difference between giving up and letting something go.

Now it was time. Aldo stopped the wagon on the plains in front of Asha, and they looked up and saw what they'd known for so long they would see. And yet they could not have imagined it would be so vast.

Around the city was a high wall of stone, mud, and timber. On the plains to the East, there was only marshland, impassable except for a thin, raised road that could not have held much more than their wagon.

"So this is why they are there," Aldo said, and he waved toward the West, where Solé was already looking.

The expanse of black tents was breathtaking. This was no common band of raiders. Horses of every breed and color frisked in the make-shift paddocks and thousands of men stood in their armor, which seemed even from this distance to shine like the moonlit face of the sea.

"So this is why you told me about tyrants," Solé said.

"This is why."

Aldo nudged Gundi's haunches, and together the three of them made their way to the edge of the marshland. They took the thin road, which was no more than an embankment of earth that must have been repaired again and again when the rains came.

They looked to the West, but the soldiers, who were far away, must have been used to the harmless sight of merchants coming and going on the small road. "Let them come," they must have thought, "for then there will be more for us to plunder."

When Gundi reached the wall of Asha, he balked. Someone was leaning over the parapet and calling to them in a strange whisper.

"Who's there?"

"Do you want to answer, Solé, or should I?"

"You do it, Papa."

Aldo lifted his voice.

"I come with something you've asked for. The truest arrows I could make, and the truest bows." And under his breath he said, though he did not know why, "and something else, the truest weapon I have."

"Then you have met one of our messengers," the voice from above said.

"Yes."

"Then you know the password."

Aldo closed his eyes and mouthed something, as though he had been practicing it for many days.

"Listen," he said.

For a long moment there was silence. Then, very slowly, the small door in the timber wall opened.

When they were within the city, many gathered around the wagon. Their faces were drawn and sleepless, and Solé saw a fear in their eyes he had never seen before.

"How long has it been like this, Papa?"

"At least since the winter. The army has made small raids on the city for months, but now the time of the great attack has come."

"It's hopeless, Papa. There are at least a thousand soldiers out there in the field. And—" he looked at the faces gathered around him. "They are so few. We are so few."

Aldo shook his head. "You must think about what I've taught you all this way. There is one thing we have that those soldiers do not."

"What, Papa? What?"

Aldo took Solé down from the driver's seat and hobbled Gundi and walked around back of the wagon. Old and tired as he was, in one motion he pulled out a bundle and let it slide to the ground. He flipped it open and revealed the arrows. Then he did it again—two bundles, five bundles, twelve—until all the arrows and bows were laid out on the ground beside the wagon.

The crowd did not move. Each face wore a look of astonishment, as though these were wonders they had never seen.

And yet Solé saw quivers and bows hanging from the clotheslines, scabbards and shields nestled in the shadows.

"Why are they so astonished, Papa? They've seen all this before." He felt his breath quicken. "What's going to happen now?"

"I don't know," Aldo said. "This is as far as my learning has taken me."

Solé watched the people of Asha step forward, one by one, toward the eagle feathers of the arrows, the imperfect curve of the bows.

"Take them." Aldo said. Solé had never heard his father's voice quiver in precisely that manner. "We have no time."

The sun was high over the mountain, and beyond the walls they could hear a clattering of steel.

"So it is coming now, then," a voice said. "Now."

Aldo and Solé had climbed to the raised platform beside the main gate of Asha, and they looked over the edge of the wall to the fields below. A figure was riding back and forth in front of the soldiers, and Solé searched his heart for any of his father's words that might calm him.

"That is Tyro," a woman said. She was dressed in homemade armor and sitting on the platform with her back to the timber wall. "Nothing will stop him. This is the last city in the West that he has not taken, and when we fall, he will cross the mountain pass and take Zuzanna, and Boacea, and all the cities to the sea."

Solé looked at his father, and his father nodded.

"I'm listening," Solé said.

"Good," the woman said. "It was Tyro's brother, Pontio, who took Olan in the East, twelve years ago, and scattered its people through the land. But Pontio is dead, and now Tyro will have it all. He will stop at nothing." The woman was shaking her head, a vacant look in her eyes. "Nothing."

"I know," Aldo said.

Solé turned toward him, and very slowly so did the woman.

"You are from Olan?" she asked.

"Yes," Aldo said, "a long time ago."

Solé knew what was coming. He would hear a part of his father's story he had never heard. His mind whirled, and he leaned against the timber fence and listened.

"When Pontio came," Aldo said, "we believed our lives could not be poorer than they were. We believed in goodness and civility, in dignity and decency, in order and pride. Pontio sent a messenger to the gates of our city, and he told us what was coming. Many of us did not believe him. But for months we had heard such threats in the land. We heard people in our own city speaking blasphemies, saying how some of us in the city had brought this upon us, because of how we lived, because of who we were. And I have had to become an old man to learn that terror comes first not with lances and swords, but with words."

Solé felt something stirring inside him. His father turned and steadied him. The woman stood up.

"So you fought Pontio, then?"

Aldo shook his head. His beard was gray around his

mouth, and it moved softly.

"No. I was never the man I wanted to be. But just once I was. When I was a young man, I tried. I spoke up. I stood on a crate in the town square and I told the crowds there was another way. They would not listen. They threw me into the dungeon, and I was still there when the city was taken. Solé's mother was a braver soul than I have ever been. She had no reason to help a strange man. But she made her way to the dungeon and found the key and released me, and together we made our way out of Olan. We never returned."

"Another way," the woman said, as though pondering something she could not explain. "I don't know what other way there might have been, and I do not know now." She gestured toward the army in the plains below. "Perhaps if that young man were here, he could tell us." Solé could see that the woman was joking, but Aldo stepped back and gave a little bow. He laid his hand on his son's shoulder.

"I have brought him to you."

The city's defenders—fathers, mothers, children—were climbing up the walls, bows slung over their shoulders, arrows in their hands.

"What do you mean, Papa?" Solé's voice was trembling. "I cannot fight this fight. I cannot."

Aldo turned and looked into his son's eyes.

"I am afraid too, my son. I have brought you here, and perhaps I will be punished for it for all eternity. Perhaps I have listened to all the wrong voices." He shook his head. "I have taught you about love, grief, power, errors, hope, and courage, but there is no teacher greater than the life we live, and perhaps that is why we are here. Perhaps we can live no more in books, in stories. Perhaps there is a seventh lesson, and perhaps it is why I did not leave you at home.

Perhaps if this lesson is not learned, there will be no home. Not for you, not for me, not for anyone."

Solé looked down from the platform and saw the youngest children of Asha. They were huddled together near the keep of the city. Their parents had gone up to the parapets, and some of them wept loudly. Others were strangely silent, and in their faces Solé saw pieces of driftwood lost on the waves of the sea.

There was no wind, and the sun shone brightly on the city. Solé looked once over the parapet, and then turned back toward his father.

"I'm not supposed to be here," he said. "Let's go back, Papa."

"We can't, Solé. For soon there would be nowhere to go."

A faint music was rising from within the city. Someone was climbing to the platform, and when she reached it she held out a bow and a quiver of arrows, but Solé did not want to take them.

"You want me to fight?" Solé asked his father.

"I told you, Solé. There is only one reason to fight. And that is to defend. In my time I have not saved your mother from illness. I have not saved the children of Olan. Nothing I have done has changed the world. It is still a story of slaughter and strife. It is still a wasteland of shadows."

"Don't talk like this, Papa. Have you brought me here just to abandon me?" The sun was beating at his neck. Someone was laying cloth armor over his shoulders, placing a cold, leather helmet on his head.

"No, Solé," Aldo said. "I am here with you. But you must use what you have learned. You must."

Suddenly the timber wall swayed. They could hear ladders clasping the parapets. Horses neighed, and below him there were strange sounds that Solé had never heard before. He was searching his father's eyes for an answer.

"I want to go home," Solé said. He closed his eyes and said it again. "I want to go home."

The music within the city had stopped. The children were silent. No one was climbing the ladders, on either side of the timber wall, and the air was heavy, as it is before a great storm.

Then they heard a voice, loud and terrible and absolutely clear.

"Citizens of Asha," the voice boomed. In an instant,

Solé knew it was the one called Tyro. "I will give you one last chance. I believe in honor and dignity. I believe in combat. Do you hear me? One last chance."

"What do you want of us?" the woman who had spoken in such despair howled out now from where she was crouching.

"Fools!" Tyro exclaimed. "I want what I have told you these many weeks. I want an opponent worthy of my sword. Worthy to stand before me. Can you hear me, cowards of Asha? Send him down through these gates to battle with me, with me alone. I have waited long enough for a battle worthy of my blood, worthy of my name. Now it is time."

No one within the walls said a word.

"They are not even going to fight," Aldo whispered. "Perhaps we have come all this way for nothing. Perhaps the gifts we brought are useless."

Solé felt something terrible stirring inside him. Love, he was saying to himself. Grief. Power. Error. Hope. Courage. He could not understand the words that were moving through him, but he could not stop them. He thought of what his father had said about hope. It is an action. It is not a promise. Then he turned and looked at the citizens of Asha clutching the bows and arrows they had brought them, and which Gundi had dragged for so long through the desert, and the cities, and the hills.

"Fools!" Tyro said again. "This is the fruit of your foolishness."

Suddenly the air seemed to hum. The sun grew dark and then there was a silence Solé could not understand.

"Arrows!" The woman on the parapet was looking upward as she shouted, and then to Solé it was as if he were crouching beside his father, long ago, covering his head as the thatched roof fell around them and the earth shook with rain.

"Papa!"

"Come, Solé. Get beneath me." His voice grew stern. "Now."

Solé had tried, for the first time, to defy his father. He threw Aldo down onto the wooden planks of the parapet and tried to cover his body. The planks quivered beneath them—thud, thud, thud—and Solé waited for a pain to pierce his back, or his shoulders, or his heart, but it did not come.

The air was silent, and he could hear new sounds

below the parapet, voices moaning as though they were lost in a deep sleep.

All was still. He felt his father's breath against his ear. It rattled strangely, and Solé closed his eyes and told himself to wake. But when he opened his eyes he knew it was all true. He knew he was there.

"Papa. Papa."

He knelt beside his father and told himself not to look at what his father's hands were clasping.

But he did.

Aldo was lying on the platform, holding his chest. The feathers of an arrow were blooming between his fingers, as though he were clasping some bird that had fallen to earth, at last, after a very long way.

"Papa, no."

"It's nothing, Solé. Go. Leave me. It's all been a mistake."

People were hurrying past them. Children were weeping in the town below, and in the distance there was a sound of men clanging swords against their wooden shields.

"Go, Solé. There's still time. What a fool I've been."

"No, Papa."

"This is not the time to learn to argue. Don't go out

there, Solé. It's all been a mistake."

Suddenly the air seemed to crack open.

"Fools!" Tyro was shouting. "Shall I do it again?"

Solé's heart swayed. Never in his eleven years had he felt a rage like this, a strange pain in his heart that seemed somehow to soothe him, to protect him, like a housefire that warms the sleeping child before he wakes.

He looked down at the faces below him, and then he looked again at his father's face. He did not know what he was saying until he said it, but he heard his own voice ring out loud and clear.

"It is I," he shouted. "I'm coming, Tyro."

Aldo looked at his son in astonishment. The woman who had come to kneel beside him seemed not to know whether to grasp Solé or let him be. In the crowd below, no one spoke.

Solé clambered down from the platform and stood before the portcullis and looked out at the horses and the great armies, vast black banners hanging above them in the sun. Tyro was swinging around on his great bay horse.

"Open it," Solé said. "Open it now."

When no one answered, Solé slid his body through the slats of the portcullis and walked out onto the field. He was so small. A strange dizziness came over him. It seemed a part of him was still standing on the parapet, watching, and that part of him did not know what to do. *What have I done?* he thought. In the distance he thought he heard Gundi braying. *Even a mule, even a mule knows the fool I am.*

But the other part of Solé walked on.

Tyro reared his horse and rode up through his ranks. He wore a long black tunic and black greaves on his shins. The crest of his helmet was a long red feather, and his face was the face of someone who had not slept in many days.

He looked Solé up and down.

"This can't be," Tyro said. Then he raised his voice toward the city. "Is this a joke? Is this how you mock the great Tyro? You shall pay for this with the blood of your children. The streets will run red with the blood of your tongues!"

He turned his horse to ride back to his ranks, but Solé shouted to him.

"Stop."

Tyro halted his horse, but he did not turn back.

"Who is this child who speaks to me? Why must I endure this mockery?"

"Give me your horse."

"What?" At this Tyro turned around to face the boy standing before him. Solé let the armor fall from his shoulders, and he slung his helmet into the dust. There was so little grass left from the grazing of the army's horses.

Tyro flared with rage. He slung his arm in the air and shouted toward his ranks.

"Archers," he screamed, "volley!"

At this word the sky darkened. Solé looked up to see a wave of arrows falling toward the city. There were screams and horrible sounds, sounds Solé had only heard in his dreams, and then again there was silence.

"Should we fire?" Someone was shouting from within the city.

Solé did not know what had given him such courage.

"No!" he shouted. "Not yet."

Tyro slung his horse around once more and rode up to Solé.

"Boy," he said, "which is all you are, you see what I can do to this city in two volleys. Can you imagine what I can do in three? In ten? Can you imagine if I loosed these men, these long-starved men, upon those storehouses? Upon those people?"

Solé made himself look into Tyro's eyes, and he told himself not to look away.

"I have asked for a worthy opponent," Tyro said, "and they send you." He lowered his voice and leaned forward in his saddle. "Perhaps you are not without courage. Perhaps. But that means little. A child can have courage because he knows nothing. Like a child standing before a great wave of the sea. But it will swallow him nonetheless. And then who will tell his story?"

He turned to go, but Solé only said again, "Give me your horse."

Tyro shook his head and laughed, looking up at the clouds darkening in the sky. "And what would you do with my horse?"

"Nothing," Solé said. "I merely wanted to know what you would say. To know who you are. I must know that before I do what I am about to do."

Tyro turned now. He lifted his chin and squinted at the boy.

"What kind of boy is this?" he said, almost as a whisper. Something stirred in him, and he seemed to be remembering something from long ago.

"I'm no one," Solé said. "I am the son of a poor merchant, and I have come a long way with my father Aldo and our mule Gundi."

Tyro felt in him the king who would have laughed at this, but no laughter came.

"Gundi," he said.

"My father is sixty years old," Solé said, "and he has come a long way to bring me here, and now I know why I am here."

Tyro's eyes widened and narrowed again. He was thinking of his own father, who had died many years ago. He was thinking of the old man's words on his deathbed, how he pulled his two sons toward him, Pontio and Tyro, and told them the prophecy of the boy who would come from a strange land, with strange gifts, with a strange glint in his eyes.

"There will be one," their father had said, "whom you cannot kill. You can kill his flesh, but you will be undone by it. Because he will have said to you that which will wake you from the sleep you call your life. And though you slay him, his words will haunt you all your days, and your life will become a silence, and your children will become that silence, and your Empire will crumble, for generation after generation will carry that shame. And shame, my sons, shame is the only thing that can bring even a dead life to its knees. Shame will undo you even if you do not know it is yours."

Tyro was staring wildly as he recalled these words. He looked back at his armies, and then he looked at the boy in front of him.

"Speak," he said.

"Very good," Solé heard himself say. "Very good."

He let loose all that had gathered in his heart in the long journey, and it seemed that he was saying words that had always been with him since the beginning.

His voice was strong, and he felt the words moving through him like a great storm.

"We fight the wrong battles in our lives, Tyro. When we fight these wrong battles, we suffer more when they are over. For we have done harm. And we are cast back to the wound in us that has no name. This is why many do not wish their battles to end. This is why many make war without cease."

Tyro again wanted to laugh, but he did not. As the boy spoke, the soldiers began to inch forward, to listen.

They were whispering to each other, relaying the words back through the ranks. On the parapets, the citizens of Asha were cupping their ears so they might hear.

"Every life is a ghost story," Solé said. "Your heart is made in your youth, by all that happens to you, by the hands of those who hold it. You can change your heart, Tyro, but only with great labor, and only by learning what it is. Many do not reach this point. Many spend their lives driven by the little fire inside them, without knowing the least bit about what it is, and how it was made, and by whom."

Tyro shook his head, but Solé kept speaking.

"What pain is making your life, Tyro?" Solé said. "Is it grief? Grief is a terrible master. We do not need to trust it to let it in. And what does it do once it's inside? It does its work. It begins to change us before we even know we are being changed. And we may only know many years later that it has been in us all awhile. It will show in our actions. In our words. We may look back at the shape our life has taken, at the harm we have done, and feel like fools. We may say, 'Grief did that. Grief was shaping my life.'"

Nothing could stop Solé. The words came from him as though they'd been written since the beginning. His body was light and his breath was crisp, even after the long way he had come.

"We fear these forces inside us, Tyro, and so we never see them. A person can become so afraid of his own life that he asks someone else to carry it. This is what a tyrant does. He makes you afraid of yourself. He tells you there is something dark and vicious in the world, some enemy always at your gates, and you do not even know that he is describing your own shadow. He may call this shadow by different names: them, those people, the enemy. But all the while he is talking about you. And because you are so afraid, because you cannot carry that fear, you ask the other to carry your shadow for you, and you make war against that other, and you seek to destroy them. But all the while you are destroying yourself." He paused. "Who is your tyrant, Tyro? Who have you let become the master of your soul?"

Very slowly Tyro slid down from his horse and stood in front of this strange boy who had come from the East.

"Who is this child?"

"Perhaps I am no child. I don't know, Tyro. But I know I must be honest with myself about what I have done. Because if I am not, there will be a terrible silence in my life, and then there will be a terrible silence in yours.

And in the terrible silences of our lives, the worst stories can grow."

Tyro said nothing.

"And what story has brought you here, Tyro? What story keeps you a secret to yourself? What does it matter? What can we do when the flag of those who do not know themselves is always the most powerful in the world?"

The banners of the army fluttered in the wind.

"We never know when despair will come," Solé said, "like raiders on the road in their dark hoods, their horse's hooves pounding like rain. These people behind me," Solé waved at the city, "they do not know. But neither do you, Tyro. And when despair comes, as it will come to you one day, Tyro, even to you, even if only when you are lying in your bed, waiting for death, then you must become, if only for a moment, like these people."

Tyro was looking beyond Solé toward the walls of the city.

"Good," Solé said. "Look at them. They may say they are in despair, but then—look, see their hands still working, still fixing an axle, still mending a fence, still brushing their children's hair as the thieves of life circle on their horses. That is hope, Tyro: not a word, not even a promise we make to ourselves. It is the thing in us that will not easily be conquered. It is the eyes opening by morning, the left foot in front of the right, the heart still choosing to say beauty.

The human heart is the only thing in this universe that can open again while knowing why it closed."

Tyro said nothing in response. A vast whisper was moving through his ranks, and Solé could feel the breath go out of the soldiers, as if they had been waiting for this moment, as if some great release were upon them.

Solé turned to them now.

"You already know," he said, "that courage is not the absence of fear. So I will not teach you that. But I can teach you this. The hardest thing to carry is a fear without a name. We may succeed in finding the right name for it, but so many lives are lost in the effort to find a name for their fear. In their haste to escape it, they give that fear the wrong name. They say they are afraid of something, of someone, when that something is only a vessel to hold their own fear. Of the world. Of themselves. We do this with our hatred, too. We do this with our wounds. We give them a name, and a face, and we say we are courageous for facing those faces. But all the while we are fighting the wrong war."

He breathed deeply. He could smell the horses and

the armor and the men.

"Tyro, with what force do you cling to your pain and call it joy? With what fear do you bang these gates? Child, what do you need?"

Solé knew he had been saying his father's words, but now he felt himself wading out into a great depth. He felt his own words rising in his life.

"Go home, soldiers. For if you destroy the home of another, you shall never have a home. And if you destroy the hope of another, you will never have hope. Those who are conquered may be conquered. In death, maybe even they will find their peace. But slayers," he said, "slayers have no shelter from themselves."

He could feel the soldiers stirring. Some laughed, some spoke, but most were silent.

Very slowly Solé took off his tunic and laid it on the ground beside him. His thin ribs showed in the sun.

"Drive your daggers into me, then. Look into the eyes of the one you kill. I still have this breath in me. And with it I will let loose a cry you can never forget. And no matter how hard your heart is, that cry will stay with you all your days. And do you know what will happen to you then? You will try not to hear it. You will close your ears, your heart. You will lie in bed with your loves, with your children, and you will hear them speak, but you will not be able to listen. You will not be able to listen. And then," Solé said, "will you be alive at all?"

Solé did not wait for an answer. He turned his back on Tyro and made his way through the city's gates and climbed to the platform and found his father.

When he saw him, he knew the vision he'd had on the road, days ago, had been true.

"No, Papa. No."

His father had broken off the end of the arrow that bloomed from his chest, and someone had propped his shoulders against the wall of the parapet. His tunic was dark and wet, and his face was pale.

"I heard it all, Solé."

"Don't talk. It's okay."

Aldo smiled. "I should have talked less and held you more."

"Don't say that, Papa."

Aldo thumbed something from Solé's lips, though nothing was there.

"What should we do?"

"I'll fetch someone to help."

"Yes," Aldo said. "Very good."

Solé began to rise, but Aldo held his arm.

"Not now, my son. Let's rest a moment together. We've had a long journey, haven't we?"

Solé knelt down again before his father. His hands were trembling. His eyes were wet.

"Yes, Papa."

"And we're here now, aren't we?"

"Yes."

Aldo rolled his eyes toward his son and smiled.

"Good," he whispered. "Very good."

Solé waited a long while before he spoke. He had felt all the strength go out of him. The children in the city below were weeping, and Solé did not want to look at what the arrows had done. He did not want to look at anything for a very long time.

"I don't know if what I said will work, Papa. I'm afraid."

Aldo held the bare shoulders of his son and pulled him down and embraced him.

"That is the message, my child. We all are."

Solé watched his father close his eyes.

"You have not yet fought your battles," Aldo said,

"but they are coming. Perhaps they will be with others. Perhaps they will be with yourself."

"I tried, Papa. I tried."

"I know." His father's voice was weakening. "Now we will learn something else."

Solé did not know what to do. His father's breath was ragged, but he spoke on.

"All this way I thought I would teach you seven lessons. But I see now why we have come on our journey. I've heard the words you've spoken, the lesson you have taught, and it has brought me something very close to peace. You have done something I never could have done. Only you could have done it, Solé. Only you."

Solé still knelt beside his father. His heart was open, and he told himself to remember his father's words, every one of them. He told himself this is why they had come this long way.

Aldo's voice was very weak from having spoken for so long. But he touched his son's face one more time and nodded.

"I have one more thing to tell you, Solé."

"Please, Papa. Yes."

Aldo opened his eyes wide and let his hand fall to his side.

"Witness it," he said.

Solé laid his face on his father's chest and listened. There was only silence. He did not know if what he had said to the soldiers would change them, and he knew very soon he would hear them moving. And he would not know if they were coming or going, not until the story had already been written.

The wind shifted in the East. A soft rain began to fall, rinsing the last sand from his father's hair.

And then, very slowly, the soldiers began to move.

ABOUT THE AUTHOR

Joseph Fasano's writing has been translated into more than a dozen languages and is celebrated around the world for its "lush drive to live, even in the darkest moments." He is the author of many books, including *The Magic Words, The Swallows of Lunetto,* and *The Last Song of the World.* His poetry prompts, which help people of all ages unlock their creativity, have been shared by millions worldwide. "Like Kafka and Rilke before him," critics have proclaimed, "this is the writer we trust to see the world as it is." Fasano is a writer for everyone on a quest, everyone with a question; as *The Massachusetts Review* has raved, this is our writer "for the living, for life."

www.ingramcontent.com/pod-product-compliance
Lightning Source LLC
Chambersburg PA
CBHW021433110726
47901CB00008B/2400